SNOWBOUND MYSTERY

Henry, Jessie, Violet, and Benny Alden venture to a cabin in the woods, where they find themselves trapped by a snowstorm. Luckily the log cabin is cozy—except for the strange noises and a secret code scratched into the closet door. As they await rescue, the Boxcar Children find themselves in the middle of another great mystery!

THE BOXCAR CHILDREN
GRAPHIC NOVELS

THE BOXCAR CHILDREN
SURPRISE ISLAND
THE YELLOW HOUSE MYSTERY
MYSTERY RANCH
MIKE'S MYSTERY
BLUE BAY MYSTERY
SNOWBOUND MYSTERY
TREE HOUSE MYSTERY
THE HAUNTED CABIN MYSTERY

Gertrude Chandler Warner's

THE BOXCAR CHILDREN
SNOWBOUND MYSTERY

Adapted by Rob M. Worley
Illustrated by Mike Dubisch

Henry Alden

Watch

Jessie Alden

Violet Alden

Benny Alden

Visit us at www.albertwhitman.com.

Adapted by Rob M. Worley
Illustrated by Mike Dubisch
Colored by Wes Hartman
Lettered by Johnny Lowe
Edited by Stephanie Hedlund
Interior layout and design by Kristen Fitzner Denton
Cover art by Mike Dubisch
Book design and packaging by Shannon Eric Denton

Library of Congress Cataloging-in-Publication Data
is available from the Library of Congress.

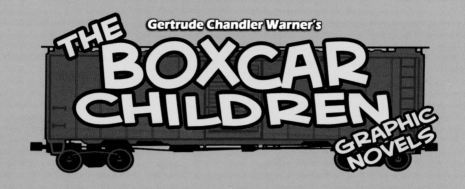

SNOWBOUND MYSTERY

Contents

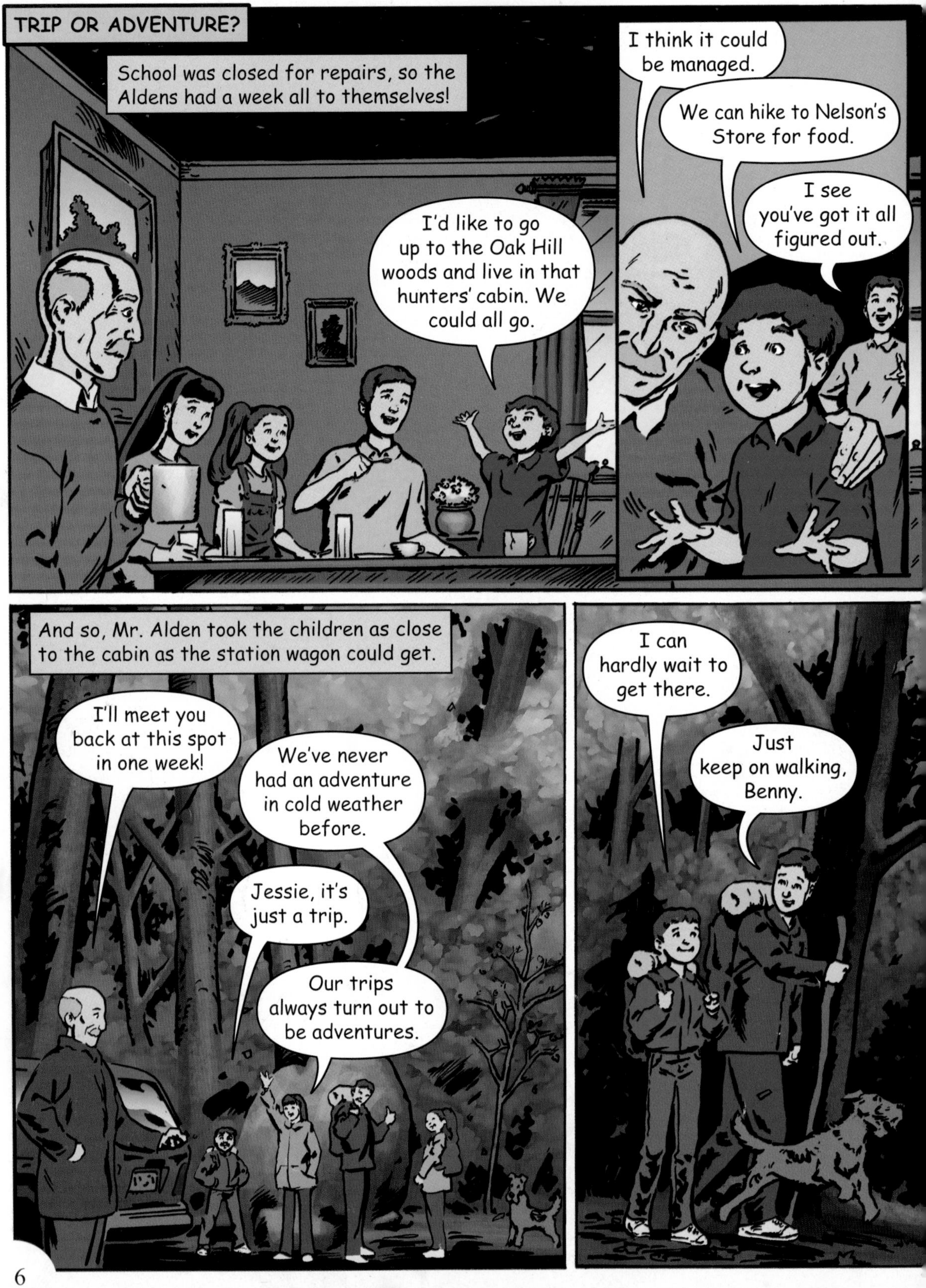
TRIP OR ADVENTURE?
School was closed for repairs, so the Aldens had a week all to themselves!
I'd like to go up to the Oak Hill woods and live in that hunters' cabin. We could all go.
I think it could be managed.
We can hike to Nelson's Store for food.
I see you've got it all figured out.
And so, Mr. Alden took the children as close to the cabin as the station wagon could get.
I'll meet you back at this spot in one week!
We've never had an adventure in cold weather before.
Jessie, it's just a trip.
Our trips always turn out to be adventures.
I can hardly wait to get there.
Just keep on walking, Benny.

Long before the family saw the cabin, Watch began to bark.

ARF! ARF!

They walked as fast as they could. Henry had the key to the door.

That window seat makes me think of the night we slept in the baker's shop. I'll sleep there!

I like the couch better. It opens out into a double bed.

You can stay this time, Watch.

You can't hurt that old couch.

It's cold.

Of course. That's fresh spring water.

7

There were two small bedrooms. Each room had two bunk beds.

Without a word, the Aldens claimed their bunks.

This must be the Visitors' Book. Grandfather told us to write our names in it.

Here's the store man, Thomas Nelson!

Here it is again. Thomas, Barbara, and...Puggsy?

They must come here a lot.

After lunch, let's take a hike to Nelson's Store.

While we're at the store, maybe we can find out if Puggsy is a boy or a girl.

Do you know the way, Benny?

No, but I guess I can find it. There is only one path.

Just then Watch smelled a rabbit.

Watch, stop!

Poor Watch stopped so fast he skidded on his side. He always obeyed Jessie.

The Nelsons must live upstairs over the store.

NELSON'S STORE

ICE

I think so, too.

We could find hickory nuts still on the ground.

We could get a lot and crack them at the cabin.

Shouldn't we go nutting another day? We still have to find Nelson's Store.

And so they walked on...

I'm Tom Nelson. I'm glad to see visitors. It's lonesome here when summer's over.

We're the Aldens.

I heard you were coming.

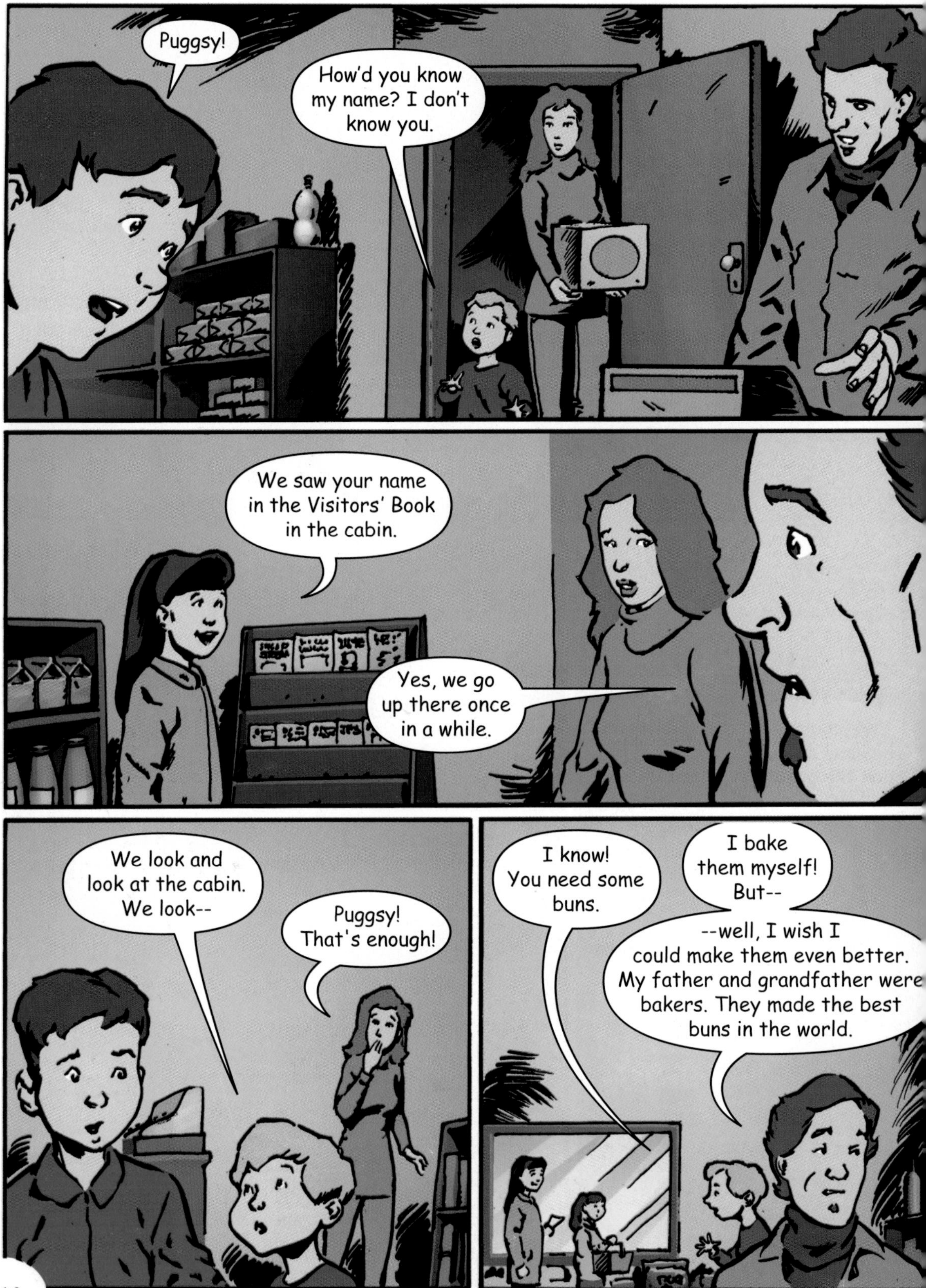

Puggsy!
How'd you know my name? I don't know you.
We saw your name in the Visitors' Book in the cabin.
Yes, we go up there once in a while.
We look and look at the cabin. We look--
Puggsy! That's enough!
I know! You need some buns.
I bake them myself! But--
--well, I wish I could make them even better. My father and grandfather were bakers. They made the best buns in the world.

On the way home...

I can't stop thinking about how Puggsy was trying to say something. And Mrs. Nelson stopped him...

There's a mystery here. I'm sure of it.

They're friendly, but it seems like they're hiding something.

When they returned to the cabin, they made supper. As it got dark, they talked about their new mystery.

I think the Nelsons come here to hunt for something.

Puggsy said "we look." But it means the same thing as hunt.

When it was really dark, they crawled into their sleeping bags. After all their hiking, they fell asleep quickly...

...but they didn't sleep for long. Watch heard a funny scratching noise.

What's that?

WOOF! WOOF!

WOOF! WOOF!

Look, Benny. The bedrooms have wooden ceilings. But the main room hasn't any ceiling at all.

There must be squirrels up there!

WOOF! WOOF! WOOF! WOOF!

Henry said he would go up on the roof in the morning. The Aldens decided to go back to sleep.

You can stop barking now, Watch.

And Watch did.

The next morning, the children set out for Nelson's Store.

We can ask Mr. Nelson about squirrels.

Farewell, you squirrels!

I don't think this weather is going to last very long.

Halfway to the store, Henry stopped suddenly. He grabbed Watch by the collar.

Then Watch gave a bark, and the deer disappeared into the woods.

At last they reached the store. They told Mr. Nelson about the squirrels.

Yes, I've heard them. Your idea of stopping up the hole in the roof is the best one.

If you let me go to the cabin, I won't hunt for anything.

No, Puggsy.

My grandfather built that cabin years ago. I suppose Puggsy thinks it's his cabin.

I like Tom Nelson. But he certainly is worried about something.

One sure thing, if they want to hide anything they'd better not take Puggsy along!

By the time the Aldens got back to the cabin, it had started to rain. Henry could not fix the roof. That night, they turned on the radio so they could hear the weather report.

...Rain tonight and clearing tomorrow. Mild weather will continue.

13

The next morning the sun came out. The children decided to gather nuts. The fat gray squirrels scolded the Aldens.

Leave the shells on. We have all day to get them off.

We should probably visit the store while we have time.

At the store...

We picked four bags of hickory nuts.

You can chop up the nutmeats and mix them with chopped apples to make a salad. It's delicious.

At the cabin, they each found stones to open the hickory nuts.

Look at us. Nut cracking with stones.

Just crack the shells now. We can pick out the nutmeats later.

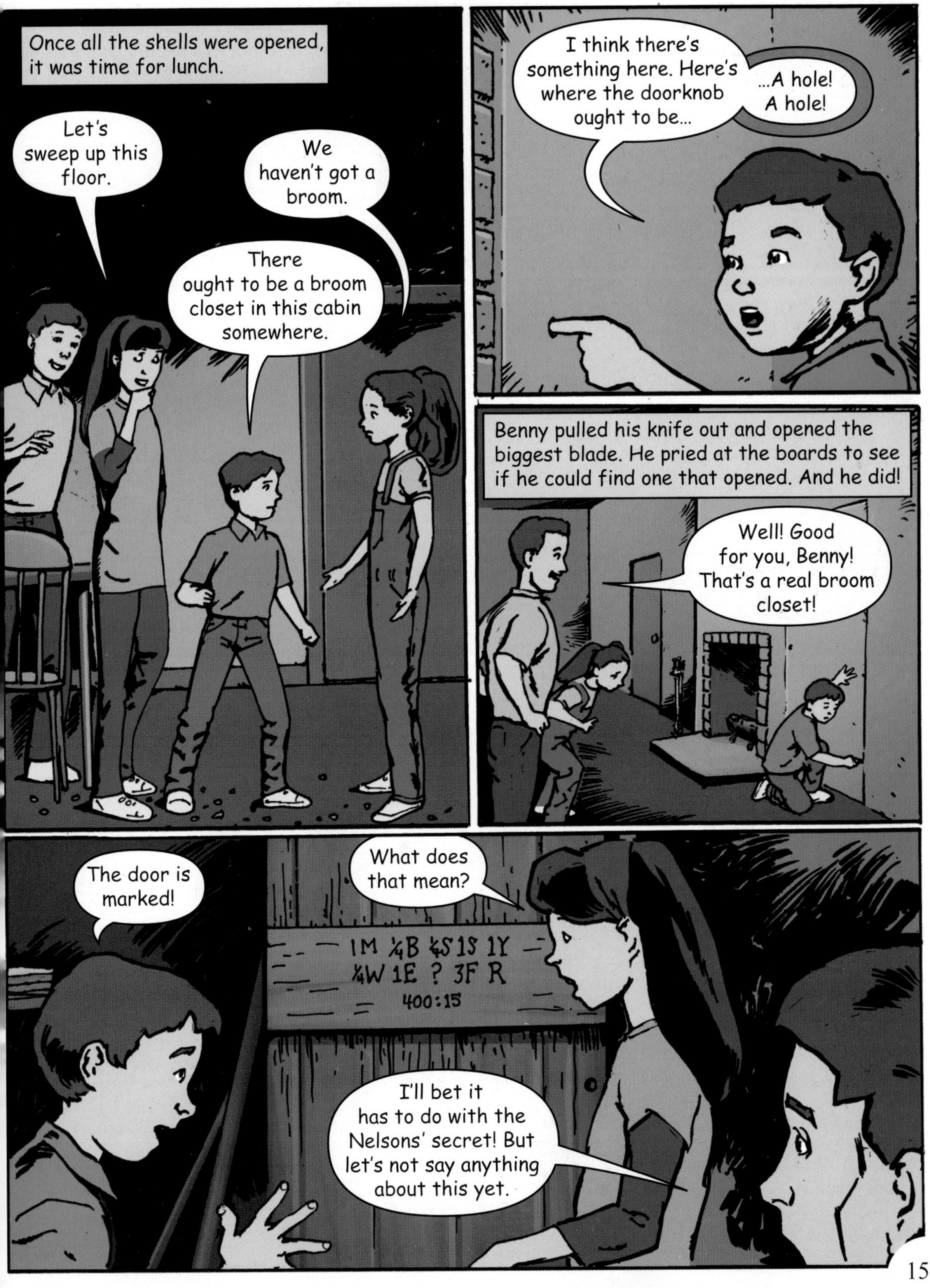

Once all the shells were opened, it was time for lunch.
Let's sweep up this floor.
We haven't got a broom.
There ought to be a broom closet in this cabin somewhere.
I think there's something here. Here's where the doorknob ought to be...
...A hole! A hole!
Benny pulled his knife out and opened the biggest blade. He pried at the boards to see if he could find one that opened. And he did!
Well! Good for you, Benny! That's a real broom closet!
The door is marked!
What does that mean?
1M ¼B ¼S 1S 1Y
¼W 1E ? 3F R
400:15
I'll bet it has to do with the Nelsons' secret! But let's not say anything about this yet.

SNOW!

The Aldens listened to the radio as they ate dinner.

A storm is coming from the southwest, but it isn't supposed to hit this area. Northern New England states should prepare for a storm.

The next day the weather had changed. The sky was very gray.

It's much colder today.

Barbara said she thought a storm was coming.

Well, never mind. The radio said the storm wouldn't hit us.

We'll have rain soon. Sometimes it rains here for days.

We're getting supplies, too.

We don't get many customers now. I'll have to move if I want to make a living.

I don't want to hurry you away, but you may get caught on the trail if snow comes.

It's snowing!

It is! Maybe it will stop as suddenly as it began.

But it didn't stop. It snowed harder.

I wouldn't like to be stuck in the snow!

We won't get stuck, Benny.

When the Aldens reached the cabin, the snow was four inches deep.

This is a very early snow. It can't last long.

Grandfather must be worrying about us. But we can't do a thing about it.

So let's enjoy it!

Henry and Benny cleared some of the snow from the cabin door.

I guess the squirrels won't have to worry for a while. I'm not going up on the roof today. I'd just like to know how big that hole is...

The next morning, the Aldens could hardly see outdoors! Snow covered the lower half of the window.

I'd call that a blizzard! I've never seen anything like it!

Benny tuned his radio to the Greenfield station to get the news.

...and Mr. James Alden wants to notify his grandchildren that they should stay in the hunters' cabin. He will get help to them as soon as he can.

I'm going to clear some snow.

I'll help you, but I'm going to wear snowshoes!

As the boys worked the snow started to melt! Soon the Aldens could see each other through the windows.

Jessie and Violet wanted to surprise the boys with lunch. But no water would come from the faucet.

I bet the pipe is frozen.

Never mind. We'll have plenty of water once we put this snow on the stove!

Isn't this good wood? It's all old and dry. Henry picked it out.

We're going right back. We had to leave a few sticks.

Then, the Aldens saw that they had visitors!

They think if they find people, they'll find something to eat, too.

The deer weren't the only visitors. The Nelsons had come to help them!

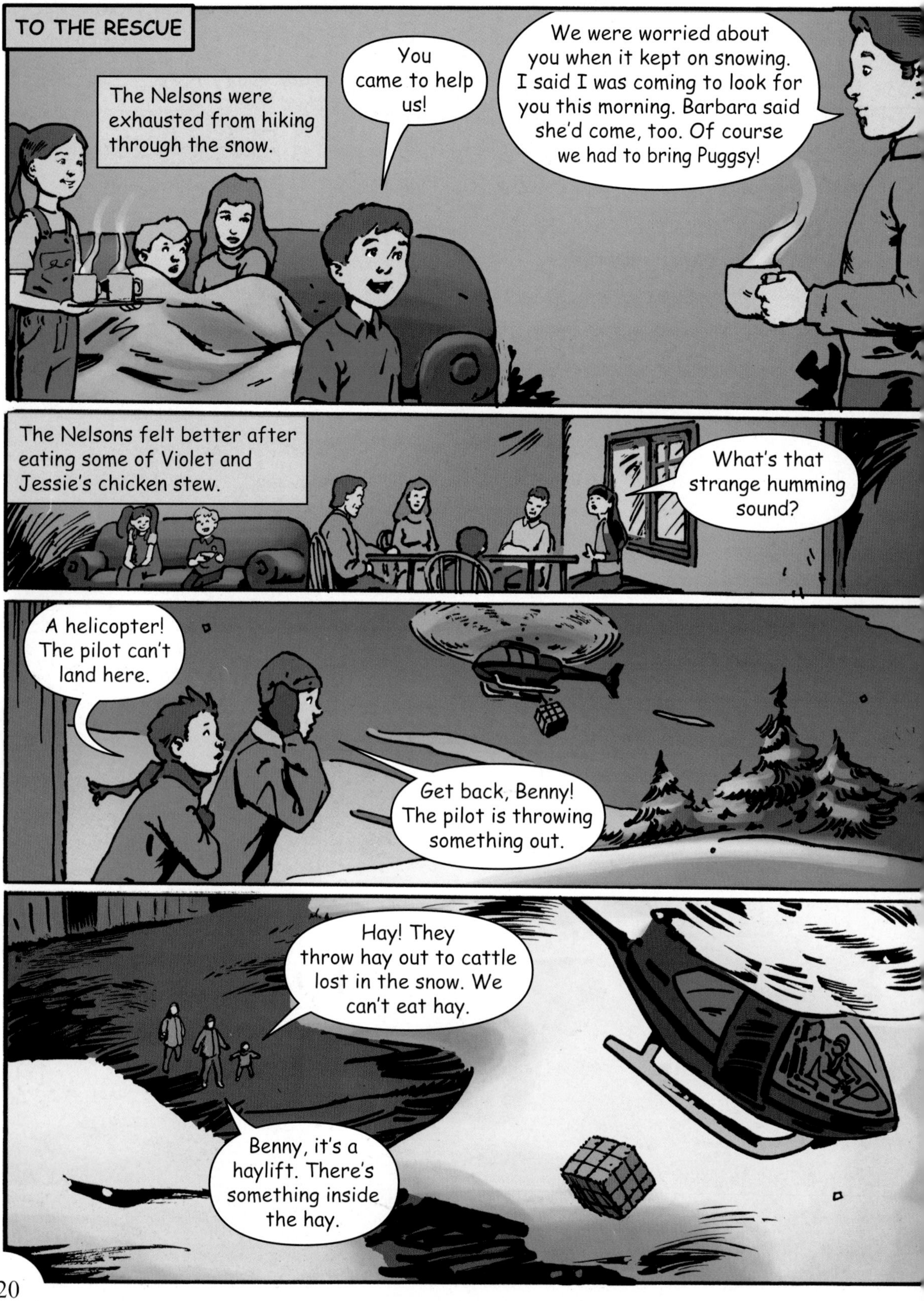
TO THE RESCUE
The Nelsons were exhausted from hiking through the snow.
You came to help us!
We were worried about you when it kept on snowing. I said I was coming to look for you this morning. Barbara said she'd come, too. Of course we had to bring Puggsy!
The Nelsons felt better after eating some of Violet and Jessie's chicken stew.
What's that strange humming sound?
A helicopter! The pilot can't land here.
Get back, Benny! The pilot is throwing something out.
Hay! They throw hay out to cattle lost in the snow. We can't eat hay.
Benny, it's a haylift. There's something inside the hay.

The boys dragged the bale of hay into the house.

There's a note from Grandfather. The Highway Department is going to get us home as planned.

He wants us to write down what we need in large letters. The helicopter pilot is coming back in two hours.

What can we write our message on?

We haven't anything big enough! And no paint or ink!

We can use this shade!

Good idea! It's the only thing in this whole cabin that's big enough.

We will have to print with something white.

I'll paint the message in water. Henry, pour salt on it while it's wet.

It's working! After the salt dries our message will be ready!

MISSING PIECE

They laid the big sign on the snow. The wind lifted the corners a little, so they put their flat nut cracking stones on each corner.

They brought the hay back outside for the deer.

Just as they finished laying the sign down, the helicopter returned. The pilot waved to the boys and soon the helicopter was gone.

3 SLEEPING BAGS. 3 NELSONS. WE'RE FINE. THANKS FOR HAY.

An hour later, the helicopter returned. It dropped the three sleeping bags that Violet had asked for.

Grandfather sent some tools as well. He wrote: "Maybe the cabin needs repairs."

They used some of the nails grandfather had sent to pick the nuts from the shells.

Tom, we know you've been looking for something in this cabin.

We don't know what it is. But we found something.

We found some letters carved on the back of the door. But we don't know what they mean.

Barbara, it's here!

Not quite.

My father and grandfather had a secret recipe for buns. The letters on the door are part of the recipe written in code.

Look, I'll show you by writing it out.

1 CUP MILK
¼ CUP BUTTER
¼ TEASPOON SUGAR
¼ TEASPOON SALT
1 YEAST CAKE
½ CUP WATER
1 EGG
???

But my father died before he told anyone the secret ingredient. When he was dying he said one word, **cabin**. I think he meant the recipe was here.

I've tried different ingredients but the buns don't taste right. I know we could make those buns famous!

That night, everyone was tired out, even Watch. After the dishes were done, they all went to bed. Even the squirrels were quiet. Until...

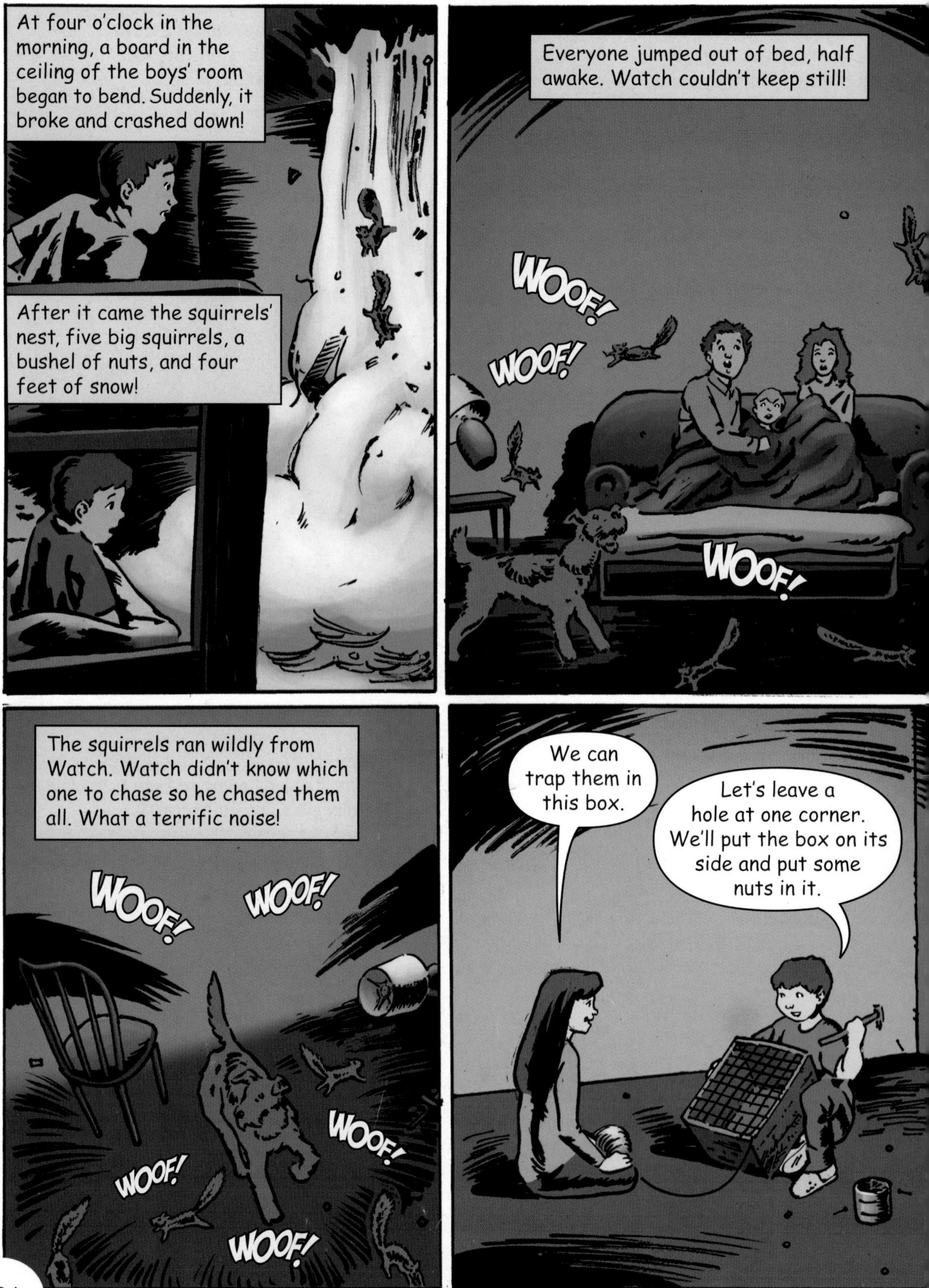
At four o'clock in the morning, a board in the ceiling of the boys' room began to bend. Suddenly, it broke and crashed down!
After it came the squirrels' nest, five big squirrels, a bushel of nuts, and four feet of snow!
Everyone jumped out of bed, half awake. Watch couldn't keep still!
WOOF!
WOOF!
WOOF!
The squirrels ran wildly from Watch. Watch didn't know which one to chase so he chased them all. What a terrific noise!
WOOF!
WOOF!
WOOF!
WOOF!
WOOF!
We can trap them in this box.
Let's leave a hole at one corner. We'll put the box on its side and put some nuts in it.

Jessie had to tie up poor Watch. With no dog, the squirrels stopped running. Everything was quiet. Slowly one squirrel went into the box.

After 20 minutes passed, they all had crawled in. Tom covered the hole and there they stayed.

After breakfast, Henry nailed the ceiling board back in place.

Look at all this paper the squirrels used for their nest.

See the pretty blue card. There's another one.

Tom! Come here!

BUNS

A miracle!

Benny, you found the missing ingredient!

A SURPRISE IN STORE

A short time later, three men from the Highway Department and a state policeman reached the cabin. They had shoveled a narrow path up the hill. They were there to bring the Aldens home.

These squirrels were in the cabin attic. If we let them go, they'll starve.

Not them! Just put your nuts on the steps and let 'em go. They'll have the nuts back in the attic before night.

I'm grateful to you, Mr. and Mrs. Nelson, for coming to help my family. I want you to stay with me until you can get back home.

We had a great adventure, Grandfather. It was a real mystery, but it's solved now.

Oh, so you did have an adventure!

Benny told Mr. Alden most of the story. Mr. Alden knew Tom wanted to open his own bakery.

I might be able to help you, but I have to try a bun first.

I can make them for dinner. I'm going to call them Benny's Buns, because he found the recipe.

At dinner, Tom served his buns hot from the oven.

These are amazing, Mr. Nelson! I never ate such delicious buns!

The next morning, Mr. Alden took Tom to the grocery store. The Alden children knew their grandfather was up to something.

Franklin's has the best meat in town. And the best groceries.

Roger Franklin's
Meats & Groceries

Do you have any sweet buns, Roger?

No, I don't carry baked things. I wish I did.

The store next to you is empty.

But I can't afford to buy it.

ONE MORE QUESTION

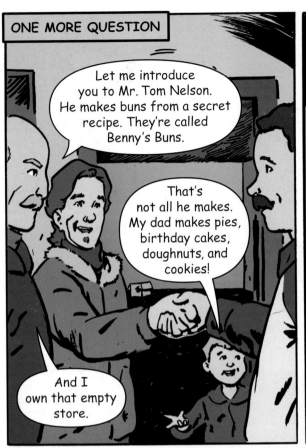

Let me introduce you to Mr. Tom Nelson. He makes buns from a secret recipe. They're called Benny's Buns.

That's not all he makes. My dad makes pies, birthday cakes, doughnuts, and cookies!

And I own that empty store.

Tom liked Roger, and Roger liked Tom.

I think we could make a go of it.

I should imagine so!

What a perfect place for a bakery.

It didn't take long to fix the store. Some carpenters came to do the heavy work. Benny noticed one special carpenter.

He always stops working when we talk about the cabin or Tom Nelson's baking.

I wonder why he's so interested?

Soon the bakery was finished. They were ready to open.

Stories about Tom, Barbara, Puggsy, and Benny were all over the news.

FRANKLIN'S STORE and BENNY'S BUNS

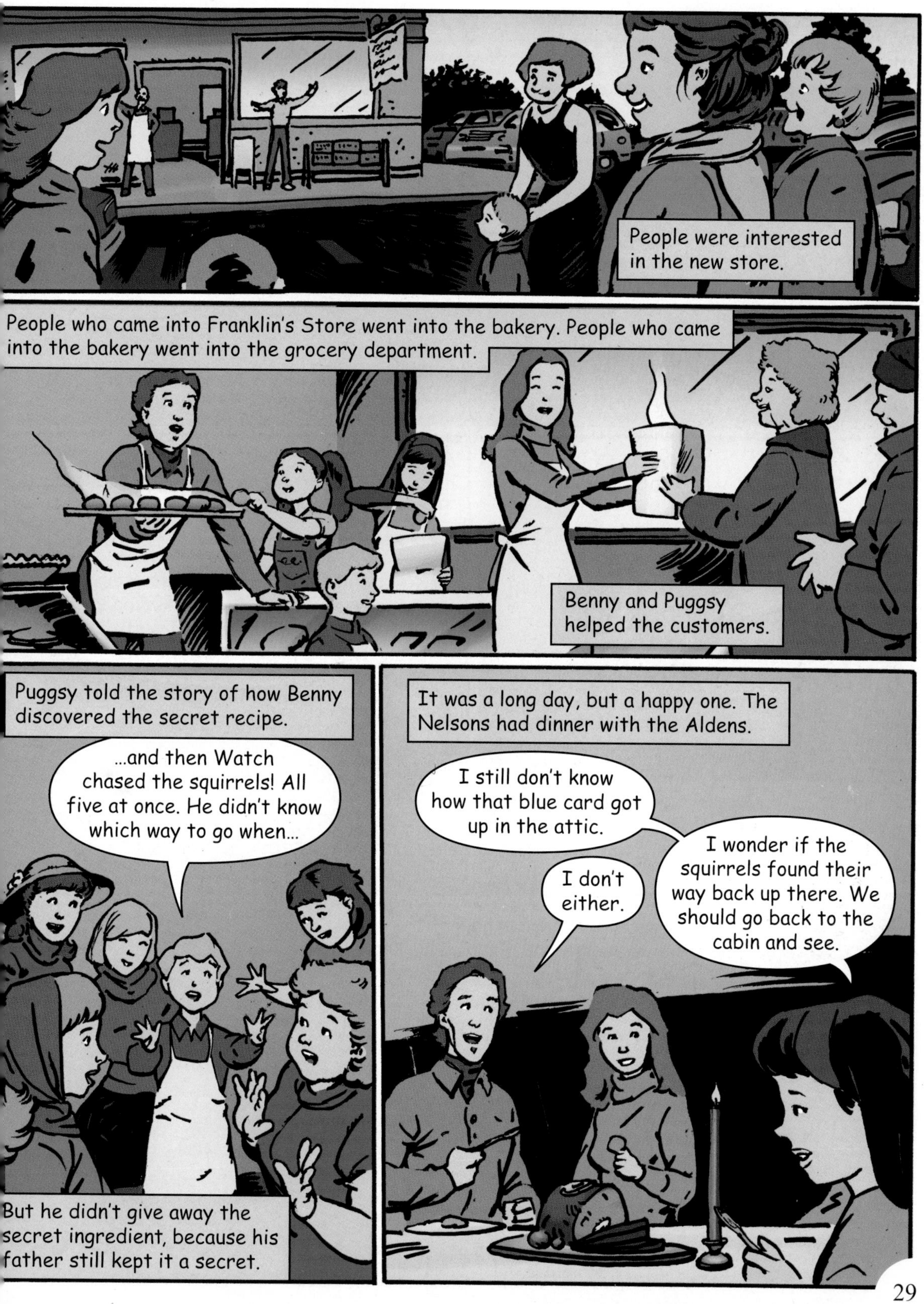
People were interested in the new store.
People who came into Franklin's Store went into the bakery. People who came into the bakery went into the grocery department.
Benny and Puggsy helped the customers.
Puggsy told the story of how Benny discovered the secret recipe.
...and then Watch chased the squirrels! All five at once. He didn't know which way to go when...
But he didn't give away the secret ingredient, because his father still kept it a secret.
It was a long day, but a happy one. The Nelsons had dinner with the Aldens.
I still don't know how that blue card got up in the attic.
I don't either.
I wonder if the squirrels found their way back up there. We should go back to the cabin and see.

One beautiful day, the Aldens and the Nelsons went up to the hunters' cabin.

That's the carpenter who worked on Franklin's Store. Remember?

Did you get all the squirrels out of the attic first?

No squirrels there! I looked.

They moved into the tree!

I'd like to talk with you before I go. My name is Don Perry. When I was working at the store, I heard how the blue recipe card was found in the attic.

After your father died, the Sportsman's Club hired me to build the ceiling in the bedrooms. They wanted to make them warmer at night.

When I was putting up the new ceiling I noticed some old recipe cards up on a roof beam. Maybe your father put them there. I left them when I nailed the attic shut.

This explains everything! I thought the ceiling had always been there. I'm glad we know.

I'm glad we got caught in the snow. If it hadn't snowed we wouldn't have found the recipe!

Well, the recipe is safe now.

And to this day, Tom and Barbara Nelson are the only ones in the world who know the recipe for Benny's Buns. And they'll never tell--until, of course, Puggsy grows up enough to keep a secret.

ABOUT THE CREATOR

Gertrude Chandler Warner was born on April 16, 1890, in Putnam, Connecticut. In 1918, Warner began teaching at Israel Putnam School. As a teacher, she discovered that many readers who liked an exciting story could not find books that were both easy and fun to read. She decided to try to meet this need. In 1942, *The Boxcar Children* was published for these readers.

Warner drew on her own experience to write *The Boxcar Children*. As a child she spent hours watching trains go by on the tracks near her family home. She often dreamed about what it would be like to live in a caboose or freight car—just as the Alden children do.

When readers asked for more Alden adventures, Warner began additional stories. While the mystery element is central to each of the books, she never thought of them as strictly juvenile mysteries. She liked to stress the Aldens' independence. Henry, Jessie, Violet, and Benny go about most of their adventures with as little adult supervision as possible—something that delights young readers.

During her lifetime, Warner received hundreds of letters from fans as she continued the Aldens' adventures, writing nineteen Boxcar Children books in all. After her death in 1979, her publisher, Albert Whitman and Company, carried on Warner's vision. Today, the Boxcar Children series has more than 100 books.